All the LOST things

Kelly Canby

Peter Pauper Press, Inc.
White Plains, New York

Published by Peter Pauper Press, Inc.
202 Mamaroneck Avenue
White Plains, New York 10601
U.S.A.

Published in the United Kingdom and Europe by Peter Pauper Press, Inc.
c/o White Pebble International
Unit 2, Plot 11 Terminus Rd.
Chichester, West Sussex PO19 8TX, UK

Library of Congress Cataloging-in-Publication Data

Canby, Kelly, author, illustrator.
All the lost things / Kelly Canby. -- First edition.
pages cm
Summary: After discovering a mysterious place of lost things,
a spunky girl named Olive gives unique gifts to her family,
saving her last present--hope--for the world.
ISBN 978-1-4413-1804-6 (hardcover : alk. paper)
[1. Gifts--Fiction. 2. Hope--Fiction. 3. Lost and found possessions--Fiction.] I. Title.
PZ7.1.C36Al 2015
[E]--dc23
2014041544
ISBN 978-1-4413-1804-6
Manufactured for Peter Pauper Press, Inc.
Printed in Hong Kong

7 6 5 4 3 2 1

Visit us at www.peterpauper.com

On her walk, Olive heard a

PECULIAR SOUND

coming from an open manhole in the street.

PUZZLED, Olive circled the manhole, scratched her head, and decided to

further by taking a peek inside.

"hello?" Olive said softly.

But there was no answer.

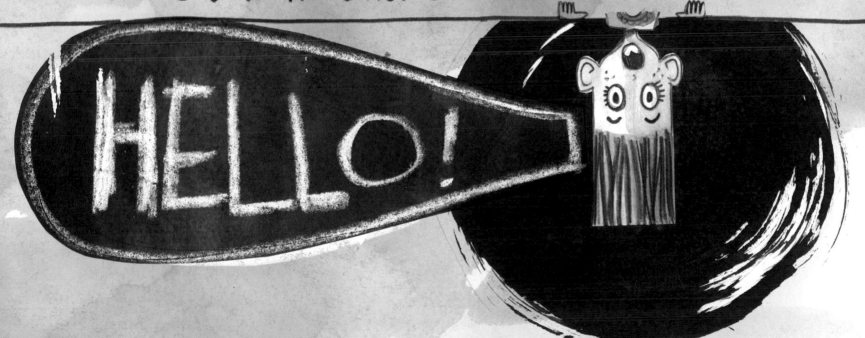

she said again. LOUDER.

Before she knew it,
Olive was climbing down
the ladder that started
from the top of the manhole
and led to...

...Well, who knew
where it led to?

CURIOSITY

had gotten the better of Olive.

At the bottom of the ladder was the peculiar sound.*

And behind the peculiar sound* were boxes.

JARS

HATS

PENCILS

SIGHT

TEETH

CAPS

GLASSES

SHIRTS

BALANCE

KEYS

TICKETS

COINS

TOKENS

RIBBONS

COMBS

VOICE

PINS

PHOTOS

CUPS

DOLLS

COURAGE

DREAMS

POWER

TIGHTS

UMBRELLAS

REMOTE CONTROLS

TEDDY BEARS

*Actually just a little old lady.

BATTLE

BOXES and BOXES and BOXES!

Intrigued, Olive asked the little old lady what all the boxes were for.

"These," said the old lady, "are ALL THE LOST THINGS from all over the city. But since no one has come looking for them in so long, feel free to take whatever you like!"

Olive scanned the BOXES
and read the labels
and looked up
and
down
the pile.

Then she gathered
five empty jars and
began to climb.

The first jar Olive filled with an enormous scoop of

This one she would take home for **Grandad**, who could never seem to remember where he'd left his glasses.

(Or anything else, for that matter.)

The second jar Olive filled with
as much

as she could

to take home for her
OLDER SISTER,

who didn't know she'd lost it,
but the rest of the family
had certainly noticed.

Next, Olive took a whopping scoop of

EYESIGHT

and filled the third jar.

This one was for DAD because (although he hadn't completely lost his yet) Olive thought it might come in handy someday.

The fourth jar Olive filled with

A gift for Mom, who could never seem to go anywhere without completely losing it.

With one jar
left to fill

LOVES

PINS

WATCHES

MYSTERY

SPOONS

IDEAS

LIGHT

Olive climbed even higher
and over even more boxes until

GYM BAGS

YOUTH

FORKS

NOTES

CHANCES

MASKS

COURAGE

SUNGLASSES

PLANS

FAITH

PHONES

she reached the very top of the pile.

And at the very top of the pile, Olive filled the last jar with a rather big,

Rather enormous,
scoop of

Olive carefully packed her bag with all five jars, thanked the little old lady, and made her way back up the long, long ladder.

Then, Olive began to walk

olive

walked to the top of the HIGHEST hill,

THEN
to the tallest
building on that
highest hill,

THEN to the very top floor of that tallest building on that highest hill and opened the jar of

HOPE

where it caught the wind
and was blown all about,

whirling and

twirling

all over the city,

before falling gently
onto the streets below
so that anyone who
may have lost it...

might find it
once again.